PowerKids Readers:
Clean and Healthy™
All Day Long

Taking My Bath

Elizabeth Vogel

The Rosen Publishing Group's
PowerKids Press™
New York

1

Published in 2001 by The Rosen Publishing Group, Inc.
29 East 21st Street, New York, NY 10010

Copyright © 2001 by The Rosen Publishing Group, Inc.

First Edition

Book Design: Danielle Primiceri
Layout: Felicity Erwin

Photo Illustrations by Thaddeus Harden

Vogel, Elizabeth.
    Taking my bath / by Elizabeth Vogel.
        p. cm.— (PowerKids Readers clean and healthy all day long)
        Summary: A young boy describes how he loves going into the bathtub with his soap, washcloth, shampoo, and rubber ducky and getting clean.
    ISBN 0-8239-5682-2 (alk. paper)
    [1. Baths— Fiction.] I. Title. II. Series.

PZ7.V8655 Tak 2000
[E]—dc21   99-045126

Manufactured in the United States of America

Contents

Every night I take a bath.
I love getting clean!

My mom fills the tub. I make sure the water feels just right.

What do I need for my bath?

- I need soap and a washcloth to clean my body.
- I need shampoo to clean my hair.
- I also need my rubber ducky, just for fun.

9

Mom says that taking a bath is important. Soap and shampoo help get rid of dirt and germs that can make me sick.

In the tub, I use the soap and washcloth to scrub my body. The soap gets my body clean.

My mom squeezes the shampoo onto my hair. She rubs it in until it makes lots of bubbles.

My mom helps me rinse
the shampoo out. We
are careful not to get any
shampoo in my eyes.

My feet are wet. I have to climb out of the tub slowly. I do not want to slip.

My mom wraps a towel around me. I am clean and dry. I love bath time!

Words to Know

TUB

RUBBER DUCKY

SHAMPOO

SOAP

TOWEL

WASHCLOTH

Here are more books to read about taking a bath:
Just a Bubble Bath (Little Critter)
by Mercer Mayer
Inchworm Press

The Book of Baths
by Karen Gray Ruelle, Lizi Boyd (illustrator)
Harcourt Brace

To learn more about taking a bath, check out this Web site:
http://www.swmed.edu/library/consumer/bathtime.htm

Index

Word Count: 170

Note to Librarians, Teachers, and Parents

PowerKids Readers are specially designed to get emergent and beginning readers excited about learning to read. Simple stories and concepts are paired with photographs of real kids in real-life situations. Spirited characters and story lines that kids can relate to help readers respond to written language by linking meaning with their own everyday experiences. Sentences are short and simple, employing a basic vocabulary of sight words, as well as new words that describe familiar things and places. Large type, clean design, and photographs corresponding directly to the text all help children to decipher meaning. Features such as a picture glossary and an index help children get the most out of PowerKids Readers. Lists of related books and Web sites encourage kids to explore other sources and to continue the process of learning. With their engaging stories and vivid photo-illustrations, PowerKids Readers inspire children with the interest and confidence to return to these books again and again. It is this rich and rewarding experience of success with language that gives children the opportunity to develop a love of reading and learning that they will carry with them throughout their lives.